Sonia Sotomayor

Supreme Court Justice / Jueza de la Corte Suprema

Zella Williams

PowerKiDS press & Editorial Buena

New York

Published in 2011 by The Rosen Publishing Group, Inc.
29 East 21st Street, New York, NY 10010

First Edition

Editor: Joanne Randolph
Book Design: Kate Laczynski
Photo Researcher: Jessica Gerweck
Spanish Translation: Eduardo Alamán

Photo Credits: Cover, p. 1 Scott Applewhite/AFP/Getty Images; p. 4–5 Jewel Samad/AFP/Getty Images; pp. 6–8 The White House via Getty Images; p. 9 Shutterstock.com; pp. 10–11, 14–15 Alex Wong/Getty Image News/Getty Images; p. 12 Doug Collier/AFP/Getty Images; pp. 13, 21 © Associated Press/AP Images; p. 16 Paul J. Richards/AFP/Getty Images; pp. 17 (top), 22 Mark Wilson/Getty Images; p. 17 (bottom) © www.iStockphoto.com/Greg Panosian; p. 18 Jared Wickerham/Getty Images; p. 19 Abby Brack/Getty Images.

Library of Congress Cataloging-in-Publication Data

Williams, Zella.
Sonia Sotomayor : Supreme court justice = Sonia Sotomayor : jueza de la corte Suprema / Zella Williams. — 1st ed.
p. cm. — (Hispanic headliners = hispanos en las noticias)
Includes index.
ISBN 978-1-4488-0711-6 (library binding)
1. Sotomayor, Sonia, 1954—Juvenile literature. 2. Hispanic American judges—Biography—Juvenile literature. 3. Judges—United States—Biography—Juvenile literature. I. Title.
KF8745.S67W553 2011
347.73'2634—dc22
[B]

2010007490

Manufactured in the United States of America

CPSIA Compliance Information: Batch #WS10PK: For Further Information contact Rosen Publishing, New York, New York at 1-800-237-9932

CONTENTS

CONTENIDO

What if someone told you that you were about to become a **Supreme Court justice**? What if he or she also told you that you would be the third woman and first Hispanic person to hold that office? Someone gave Sonia Sotomayor just such news in 2009. Getting to this point was not easy, though. She had to work hard.

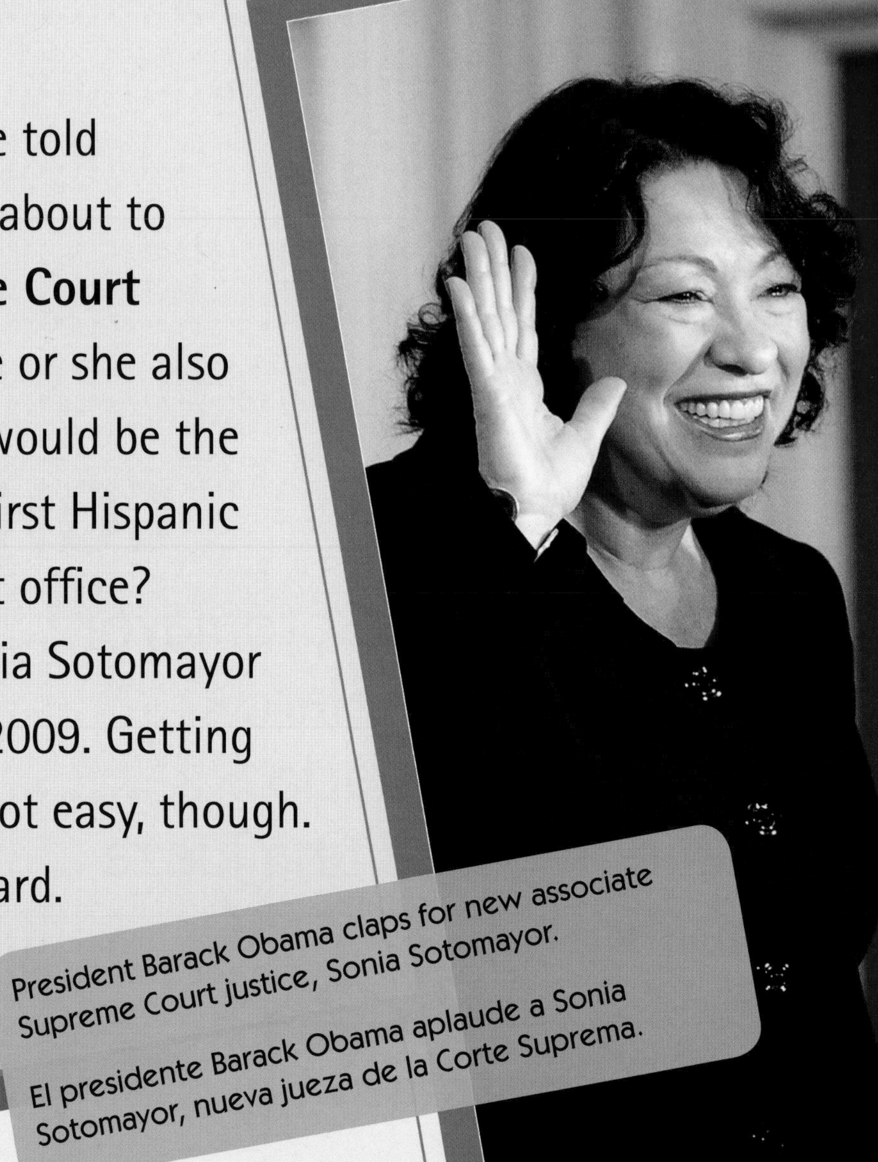

President Barack Obama claps for new associate Supreme Court justice, Sonia Sotomayor.

El presidente Barack Obama aplaude a Sonia Sotomayor, nueva jueza de la Corte Suprema.

¿Qué harías si te dijeran que vas a ser Juez de la **Corte Suprema**? ¿Y qué pasaría si te dijeran que serás únicamente la tercera mujer, y la primera persona hispana en este trabajo? Esa es la noticia que recibió Sonia Sotomayor en 2009. Pero llegar a este punto no fue fácil. Sotomayor tuvo que trabajar arduamente.

Sonia Sotomayor was born in the Bronx, New York, on June 25, 1954. Her parents, Juan and Celina Baez Sotomayor, were born in Puerto Rico. Juan Sotomayor worked as a toolmaker. Celina worked as a nurse. Sonia's father spoke only Spanish, so she grew up in a bilingual household.

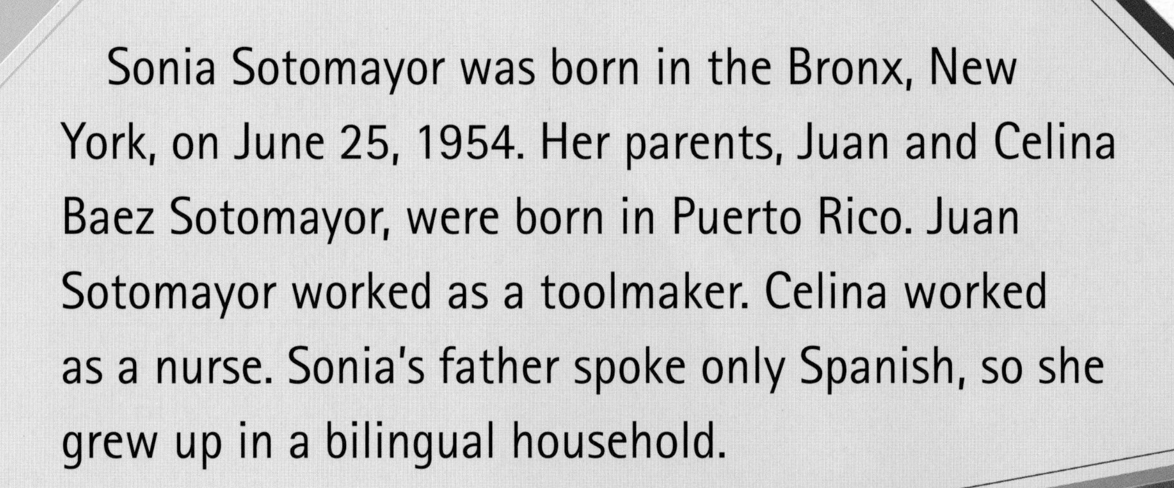

Here a young Sonia is pictured with her mother and father, Celina and Juan.

Aquí vemos a Sotomayor de niña con su madre, Celina, y su padre, Juan.

Sonia Sotomayor nació en el Bronx, Nueva York, el 25 de junio de 1954. Sus padres, Juan y Celina Baez Sotomayor, nacieron en Puerto Rico. Juan Sotomayor trabajaba haciendo herramientas. Celina era enfermera. El papá sólo hablaba español, por lo que Sotomayor creció en un hogar bilingüe.

Sonia Sotomayor is six or seven years old here.

En esta fotografía, Sotomayor tendría unos seis o siete años.

Sonia and her mother have stayed close through the years.

Sotomayor siempre ha tenido una relación muy cercana con su madre.

After Juan Sotomayor's death, Celina raised Sonia and her brother, Juan, on her own. Sonia worked hard at her studies. She graduated from Cardinal Spellman High School as the **valedictorian** in 1972. She studied history at Princeton University. She then received her law degree from Yale Law School in 1979.

Sonia Sotomayor is shown here at her eighth grade graduation.

Aquí vemos a Sotomayor en su graduación de octavo grado.

Sotomayor went to Princeton University, shown here.

En esta fotografía vemos la Universidad de Princeton a la que asistió Sotomayor.

Tras la muerte de su esposo, Celina se encargó, por sí misma, de Sonia y su hermano Juan. Sonia fue una excelente estudiante. En 1972 se graduó con honores en la escuela secundaria Cardinal Spellman. Luego estudió historia en la universidad de Princeton. En 1979, obtuvo su título de abogada en la escuela de derecho de la Universidad de Yale.

After earning her law degree, Sonia Sotomayor took a job as assistant district attorney in New York City. In this job, she **prosecuted** people who had committed small crimes and people who had hurt and killed others. In 1984, she left the district attorney's office and spent eight years in private practice.

Working in private practice was a big change for Sotomayor.

Trabajar en el sector privado fue un gran cambio para Sotomayor.

Tras obtener su título de abogada, Sotomayor trabajó como asistente del fiscal en la ciudad de Nueva York. En este trabajo **enjuició** a personas que habían cometido crímenes. En 1984, Sotomayor dejó su trabajo, y pasó ocho años trabajando como abogada en el sector privado.

In 1992, Sonia Sotomayor became a judge of the Federal District Court for the Southern District of New York. It was her job to listen to and make decisions on cases presented by lawyers. She is remembered most for a decision she made in 1995. This decision ended a 232-day Major League Baseball strike.

George Steinbrenner, an owner of the Yankees, is shown talking about the baseball strike in 1994.

George Steinbrenner, dueño de los Yankees de Nueva York, durante la huelga de 1994.

Here Sotomayor stands in her office when she was a federal court judge.

Sotomayor en su oficina durante su tiempo como Jueza Federal de Distrito.

En 1992, Sotomayor se convirtió en Jueza Federal del Distrito Sur de Nueva York. Su trabajo era escuchar los casos presentados por los abogados y tomar una decisión. Una de sus decisiones más famosas en esa época fue la de 1995. Su decisión terminó con la huelga de los jugadores profesionales de béisbol que había durado 232 días.

What was the next stop in Sonia Sotomayor's promising career? She became a judge of the U.S. Court of **Appeals** for the Second Circuit in 1998. She heard appeals on more than 3,000 cases and wrote nearly 400 majority opinions. A majority opinion is one on which most members of that court agree.

Sonia Sotomayor worked hard in her job as a judge for the U.S. Court of Appeals.

Sotomayor trabajó intensamente en su puesto como jueza de la Corte de Apelaciones de los E.E.U.U.

¿Cuál sería el siguiente paso en la carrera de Sonia Sotomayor? En 1998 se convirtió en jueza del segundo circuito de la Corte de **Apelaciones** de los Estados Unidos. Sotomayor escuchó más de 3,000 apelaciones y dictó mas de 400 opiniones de mayoría, en las que la mayoría de los miembros de la corte estuvieron de acuerdo.

In May 2009, Sonia Sotomayor was **nominated** by President Barack Obama to fill a seat on the Supreme Court. As an associate justice on this court, it would be her job to make sure decisions by lower courts upheld the **Constitution**. She was approved as associate Supreme Court justice in August 2009.

Sotomayor was sworn in as a Supreme Court justice in August 2009.

Sotomayor realiza el juramento como Jueza de la Corte Suprema de Justicia en Agosto de 2009.

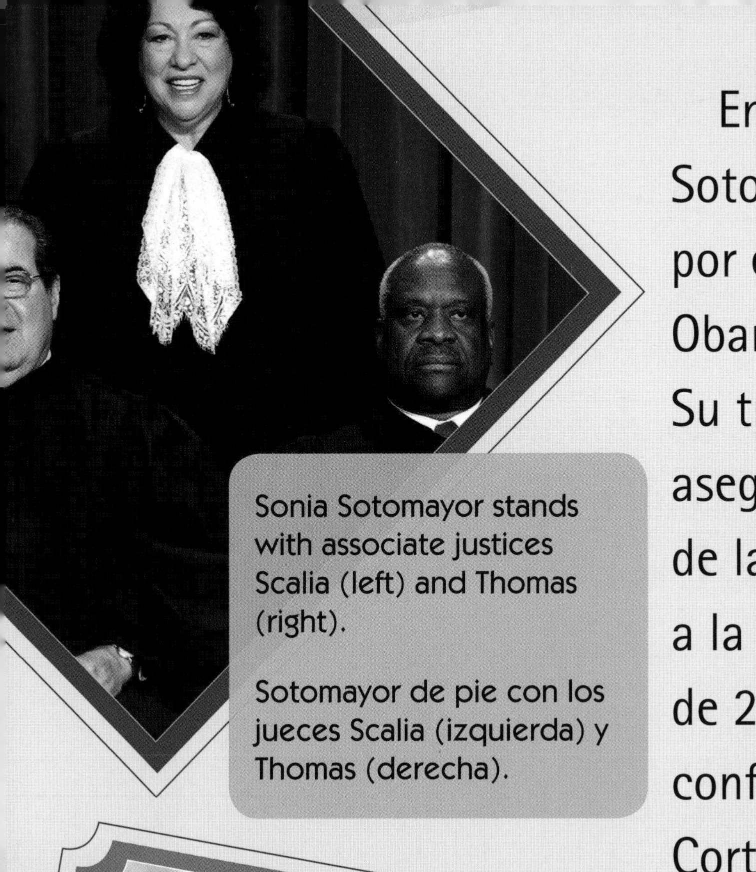

Sonia Sotomayor stands with associate justices Scalia (left) and Thomas (right).

Sotomayor de pie con los jueces Scalia (izquierda) y Thomas (derecha).

En mayo 2009, Sonia Sotomayor fue **nominada** por el presidente Barack Obama para la Corte Suprema. Su trabajo en esta corte es asegurarse que las decisiones de las cortes bajas se ajusten a la **Constitución**. En agosto de 2009, Sotomayor fue confirmada como Jueza de la Corte Suprema.

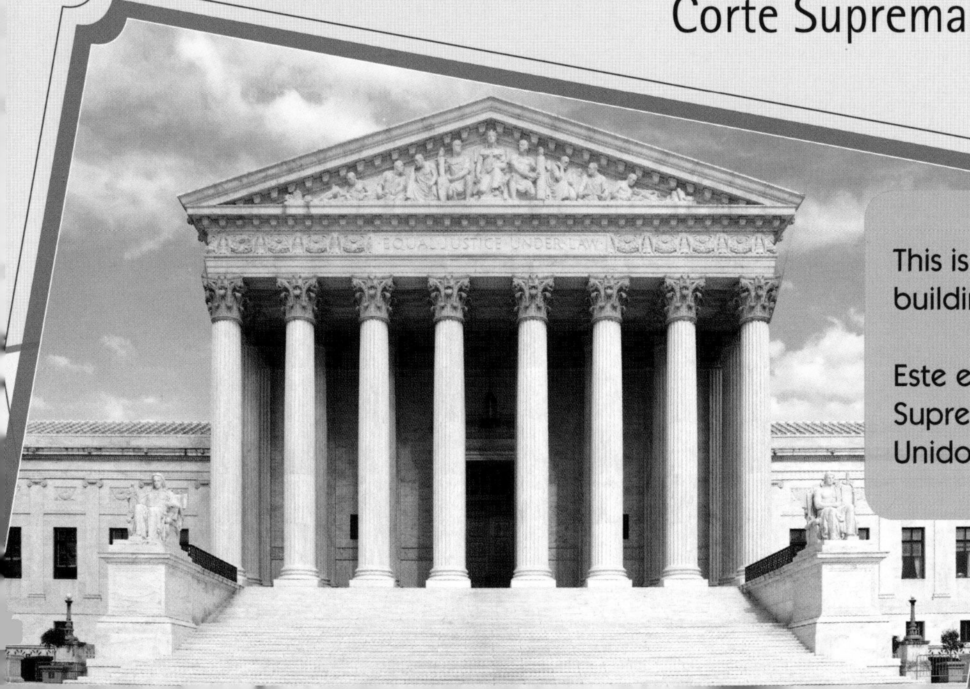

This is the U.S. Supreme Court building, in Washington, D.C.

Este es el edificio de la Corte Suprema de los Estados Unidos, en Washington, D.C.

Sonia Sotomayor has done more than just hear cases. In 1976, she married Kevin Noonan. However, after about six years their marriage ended. She worked as an adjunct, or part-time, professor at New York University from 1998 to 2007. She also began teaching law students at Columbia University in 1999.

Sotomayor is a baseball fan. She takes the mound with New York Yankee Jorge Posada here.

Sotomayor es aficionada al béisbol. Aquí camina con Jorge Posada de los Yankees.

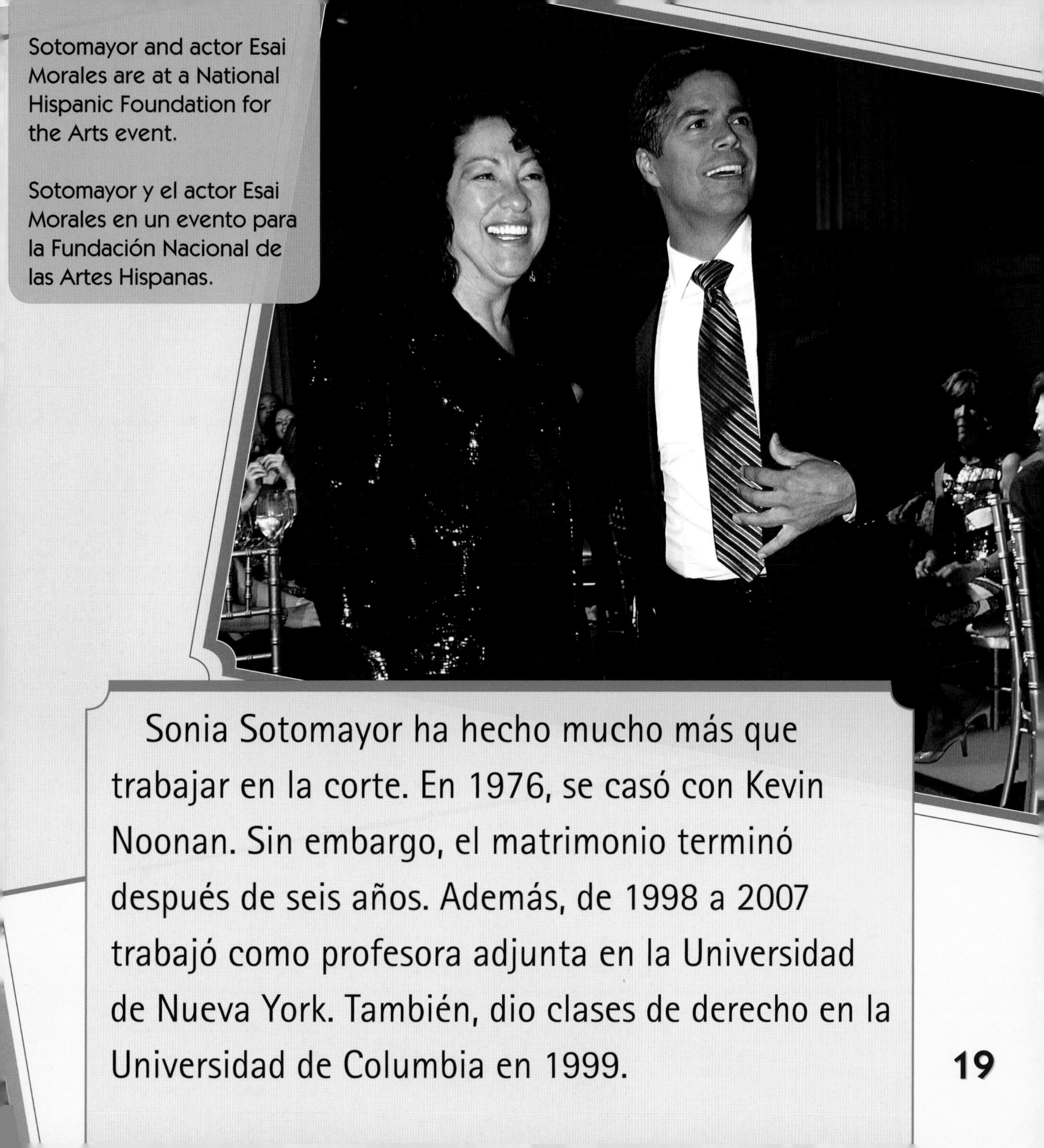

Sotomayor and actor Esai Morales are at a National Hispanic Foundation for the Arts event.

Sotomayor y el actor Esai Morales en un evento para la Fundación Nacional de las Artes Hispanas.

Sonia Sotomayor ha hecho mucho más que trabajar en la corte. En 1976, se casó con Kevin Noonan. Sin embargo, el matrimonio terminó después de seis años. Además, de 1998 a 2007 trabajó como profesora adjunta en la Universidad de Nueva York. También, dio clases de derecho en la Universidad de Columbia en 1999.

Sonia Sotomayor has always worked hard to do well. In 1976, while she was in college, she won the Pyne Prize because of that work. She has **honorary degrees** from many colleges and universities, including Princeton and Lehman College. She has also won awards for her hard work as a Latina professional.

Sotomayor speaks at an event held in her honor by the U.S. Court of Appeals judges in 2009.

Sotomayor habla en un evento en honor de los jueces de la Corte de Apelaciones de E.E.U.U. en 2009

Sotomayor ha trabajado arduamente. En 1976, cuando estaba en la universidad, ganó el Premio Pyne. Además, Sotomayor tiene **títulos honorarios** de varios colegios y universidades, entre ellos, los de la Universidad de Princeton y Lehman College. Sotomayor también ha ganado premios por su trabajo como profesionista latina.

As a justice of the Supreme Court, Sotomayor has a job that most judges only dream about. What will happen in the years to come? Only time will tell. We can hope that she judges cases fairly and upholds the U.S. Constitution. It is a big job, but Sonia Sotomayor has shown that she is not afraid to work hard.

Como jueza de la Corte Suprema, Sotomayor tiene un trabajo de ensueño. ¿Qué le espera en el futuro? Sólo el tiempo lo dirá. Sólo podemos esperar que tome decisiones justas y haga valer la Constitución. Es un trabajo muy grande, pero Sotomayor ha demostrado que no tiene miedo de trabajar muy duro.

GLOSSARY

appeals (uh-PEELZ) Asking judges in higher courts to take a second look at legal decisions.

Constitution (kon-stih-TOO-shun) The basic rules by which the United States is governed.

honorary degrees (AH-neh-rer-ree duh-GREEZ) Ranks or titles given by colleges or universities to honor, or recognize, people for what they have done.

justice (JUS-tis) Another word for a judge.

nominated (NAH-muh-nayt-ed) Suggested for an award or a position.

prosecuted (PRAH-sih-kyoot-ed) Took legal action against someone for the purpose of punishment.

Supreme Court (suh-PREEM KORT) The highest court in the United States.

valedictorian (va-luh-dik-TOR-ee-un) The student with the highest grades and who generally gives a speech at graduation.

GLOSARIO

apelaciones (las) Pedir a los jueces de las cortes superiores que revisen una decisión legal.

Constitución (la) Documento con las reglas básicas con las que se gobierna un país.

Corte Suprema (la) La corte más alta en los Estados Unidos.

enjuiciar Tomar acción legal contra una persona.

nominación (la) Sugerir, o ser sugerido, para ocupar una posición o recibir un premio.

títulos honorarios (los) Las distinciones otorgadas por colegios o universidades para honrar, o reconocer, a una persona.

INDEX

ÍNDICE

WEB SITES / PÁGINAS DE INTERNET

Due to the changing nature of Internet links, PowerKids Press and Editorial Buenas Letras have developed an online list of Web sites related to the subject of this book. This site is updated regularly. Please use this link to access the list: www.powerkidslinks.com/hh/sotomayor/